Little, Brown and Company

Hachette Book Group
1290 Avenue of the Americas, New York, NY 10104
Visit our website at www.lb-kids.com

Little, Brown and Company is a division of Hachette Book Group, Inc.
The Little, Brown name and logo are trademarks of Hachette Book Group, Inc.

The publisher is not responsible for websites (or their content) that are not owned by the publisher.

First Edition: September 2013

Library of Congress Cataloging-in-Publication Data

London, Olivia.
    Welcome to the Crystal Empire! / by Olivia London. — First edition.
        pages cm. — (My little pony)
    ISBN 978-0-316-22824-4
    I. Title.
    PZ7.L8434Wel 2013
    [E]—dc23

                                                                              2013007283

                        10 9 8 7 6

                                        CW

                        Printed in the United States of America

My Little Pony™

Welcome to the Crystal Empire!

By Olivia London

Ⓛ Ⓑ

LITTLE, BROWN AND COMPANY

New York Boston

"Hey, Spike," says Twilight Sparkle as she enters the library. "When did that scroll arrive?"

"Just a second ago," he answers, handing it to her.
"It's from Princess Cadance and Shining Armor!" Twilight cries in excitement.

Dear Twilight Sparkle,

Shining Armor and I would like to invite you to the Crystal Empire. Please join us for the Crystal Faire, which is taking place at the end of the week. We'd love for you to come a few days early so we can show you around our kingdom. Since your last visit, the Crystal ponies have been working hard to bring the sparkle back to the Empire. Your room in the castle is already made up. You'll even have your very own library!

With much love,

Princess Cadance
& Shining Armor

"Did you hear that, Spike?" Twilight says happily. "They want me to come visit for the Crystal Faire!"

"It should be much more fun this time around," jokes Spike. "You know, now that you don't have to save the Empire from an evil Unicorn."

"That's for sure," Twilight agrees. "Not to mention that this time there will be no test from Princess Celestia. Do you remember how nervous I was?"

"Twilight, *everypony* remembers how nervous you were," Spike answers.

"Hmm, I guess I should start packing!" says Twilight. "Should I bring my books and my quills, just in case?"

"Promise you'll write to all of us about your trip?" Spike asks, jumping on top of Twilight's bag.

"I promise! Tomorrow, I'll say good-bye to all my friends, and then it's off to the Crystal Empire!"

The next morning, Twilight meets her friends in the town square to say good-bye.

"Ooh, I can't wait to hear all about the party!" Pinkie Pie exclaims, bouncing up and down.

"Well, it's not exactly a party—it's a Faire," Twilight corrects her.

"Y'all be careful now, ya hear?" Applejack says.

"Are you sure you don't need company?" Rarity asks. "The Crystal Empire is gorgeous—I'm just *dying* to see it again!"

"I'm sorry, Rarity, but they invited only me," Twilight replies. "It's the first time since the wedding that we'll be together as a family. You can come with me next time, okay? Oh, and Rarity, would you check in on Spike for me?"

"Of course," Rarity says.

"Have fun, Twilight!" Rainbow Dash calls out.

"Write to us!" Fluttershy offers.

"I will, I promise. See you soon, everypony!"

With that, Twilight Sparkle sets off on her journey to the Crystal Empire.

Twilight settles into her seat on the train and stares out the window, thinking about the last time she rode this same train. She was on her way to save the Crystal Empire from the evil Unicorn, King Sombra.

"Boy, a lot has changed since my last trip," Twilight remarks to herself, taking out her quill and a piece of parchment.

Dear Spike,

I know I just left Ponyville this morning, but I miss you already! Riding the train to the Crystal Empire is bringing back so many memories. It's hard to believe there was a time when we didn't know the Crystal Empire even existed. I'm still amazed that Princess Celestia trusted me to help protect it. Thank goodness I had you there with me. Otherwise, I never would have succeeded. I'm looking forward to seeing the Empire back in its prime—the way it used to be before it was overtaken. I can't wait to arrive and be able to tell you all about it. More later!

XOXO,
Twilight Sparkle

"Shining Armor!" Twilight cries out, seeing her brother waiting for her by the train station.

"Twily, it's so great to see you!" Shining Armor says, overjoyed. "Welcome back to the Crystal Empire. This time I promise we're actually going to have some fun."

When they arrive at the castle, Princess Cadance greets Twilight with a warm embrace.

"Sunshine, sunshine, ladybug's awake. Clap your hooves and do a little shake!" the ponies sing out in unison, clapping their hooves.

"It's wonderful to see you, Twilight," Princess Cadance says. "Thank you for coming to visit us. I'm looking forward to showing you around our Empire—now that everything is back to normal."

"It's so great to be here," Twilight replies. "I can't wait!"

Princess Cadance and Shining Armor show Twilight to her room so she can settle in.

"This room is huge!" Twilight exclaims.

"Our home is your home," Shining Armor replies. "Don't forget to check out the library. We'll be back in a little while to take you into town."

After spending some time reading up on the history of the Crystal Empire, Twilight decides to write another letter home.

Dear Applejack,
   I'm in a room so big it could probably fit all of Sweet Apple Acres! Okay, well, maybe not quite that big....I've just been reading through some of the Crystal Empire's history. It still amazes me that one thousand years ago, King Sombra overtook the Empire. Thankfully, he was overthrown and banished, but before he left he cast a curse on the Empire, which caused it to disappear! That's why no one knew it existed!
   Princess Celestia told me that if the Crystal Empire is filled with love and hope, those feelings are reflected across all of Equestria. But if hatred and fear take hold, they spread across Equestria, too. Pretty heavy, huh? I'll write more later, I promise! Say howdy to everypony for me!
                              Always,
                              Twilight

"We thought we'd just take a walk around the center of town first," Shining Armor says to his sister.

"Sounds great!" Twilight replies. "When is the Crystal Faire?"

"It's in two days," Princess Cadance says. "The Crystal ponies have been preparing for it all week long. It is the first real Crystal Faire since the Empire was reinstated, so it's a very special occasion."

"The Crystal ponies have a long and cultured history," Shining Armor adds. "A thousand years is a lot of time to make up for!"

Dear Fluttershy,

   The kingdom is so...so sparkly! All the Crystal ponies are really shiny now that they've got their Empire back. Did you know that when meeting with special guests, it's traditional for rulers of the Crystal Empire to weave crystals into their manes? It's called a special ceremonial headdress! Maybe we'll get to see Princess Cadance wear one sometime. Anyway, it was fun seeing the preparations for the Crystal Faire. It reminded me of when we were all here trying to put the Faire together when the Empire was in danger. I'm so lucky to have you ponies as my friends! Time to go to dinner now, more later.

                              Love,
                              Twilight Sparkle

"Rise and shine!" Shining Armor calls into Twilight's room the next morning.

"I'm up, I'm up," she replies sleepily.

"Come on and get ready. We're going somewhere special this morning!" he announces.

"Hmm," Twilight says to herself. "I wonder where. . . ."

Dear Rainbow Dash,
    Today was the best day ever! We went to a jousting match. It was
so exciting—you would have loved it. The Crystal ponies have ancient,
intricate sets of armor and an enormous stadium. It reminded me of
when we were putting together the Crystal Faire. Next time, I promise
you'll all come with me and we'll go to a match. I hope all is well in
Ponyville! I'll write again soon.

                                        Always,
                                        Twilight Sparkle

It's the day of the Crystal Faire, and Twilight Sparkle is bursting with excitement!

"Twily, it's time!" Shining Armor calls to her.

When they reach the town square, the Faire is just beginning and the place is filling quickly with Crystal ponies from all over the Empire.

"You can really feel the love and light spreading," Twilight remarks.

"That is the purpose of the Faire," Princess Cadance offers in agreement.

"Yes, I remember!" Twilight replies. "The light and love of the ponies power the Crystal Heart, which protects the Empire from harm! This time I hope the real Crystal Heart is on display."

"Thanks to you and your friends, Twilight, the Crystal Heart is here to stay," Princess Cadance replies.

"Shall we go join in the activities?" Shining Armor says, heading for the Crystal berries booth.

Dear Pinkie Pie,

   Today was the Crystal Faire! It was full of colorful tents and booths with games, fortune-telling, crafts, a petting zoo, and tons of food! They had every kind of pie imaginable! Crystal Empire Berry Pie, Crystal Apple Pie, Crystal Peach Pie, Crystal Chocolate Pie—you name it! And this time, the real Crystal Heart was there, and it was spectacular! All the love and happiness from the ponies lit it up, and it shot rainbow sparkles into the air! Next Faire, you're all coming with me. I can't wait to come home and tell you about it.

XOXO,

Twilight Sparkle

P.S. I tried to play the flügelhorn, but I think I still need some practice. . . . Next time, you'll have to show me how it's done!

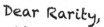

Dear Rarity,

We went to the most luxurious spa this afternoon. You would have loved it! They have a special pool called the Crystal Mud Bath that relaxes your body and rejuvenates your coat. Speaking of sparkly coats, I also spent time talking to lots of Crystal ponies. They are all so much happier now that the Empire is safe. Do you remember when we were here last time? Their coats were so dull because King Sombra had erased their memories and stripped them of their love and light. Did you know it's that special magic that makes their coats sparkle so brightly? Next time we come here, I promise you'll have time to go into some of the fashion boutiques—I just know you could make something fabulous with their shiny crystal fabric. See you soon—I'll be home tomorrow!

Love always,
Twilight Sparkle

When morning comes, it's time for Twilight to say good-bye to Shining Armor and Princess Cadance.

"Thank you so much for having me," Twilight says, getting ready to board the train. "I had the most amazing visit!"

"It was our pleasure," Princess Cadance replies.

"Don't be a stranger, okay?" Shining Armor says, giving Twilight a hug.

Dear Princess Celestia,
   My trip has made me think a lot about what happened when the Empire needed saving. I wanted to thank you for trusting me. I understand now more than ever how special the Crystal Empire is and how important it was to make sure that King Sombra did not overtake it again. It was a huge task, and I'm eternally grateful that you had faith in my ability to find the Crystal Heart and return it to the ponies of the Crystal Empire. And thank you for letting my friends come with me—sometimes we all need a little help, and I couldn't have saved the Crystal Empire without theirs. I'm so excited to go back with them soon!
                    Your faithful student,
                    Twilight Sparkle

"It's so great to be home!" Twilight Sparkle says, giving hugs to all her friends. "I had such a wonderful time, but I missed you ponies."

"We missed you, too, Twilight!" they all say happily.

Twilight looks around at everypony. "You really are my very best friends."